For Sofía and Mateo, and their many, many questions – A.M.

For my dear Nora – C.V.

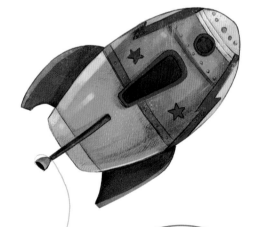

THiS BOOK BELONGS TO

_____

The illustrations in this book were created using coloured pencils and digital methods.

First published in 2022 by Floris Books. Text © 2022 Amy B. Moreno. Illustrations © 2022 Carlos Vélez. Amy B. Moreno and Carlos Vélez have asserted their right under the Copyright, Designs and Patent Act 1988 to be identified as the Author and Illustrator of this Work. All rights reserved
No part of this book may be reproduced without the prior permission of Floris Books, Edinburgh
www.florisbooks.co.uk British Library CIP data available. ISBN 978-178250-776-5
Printed in China through Imago

FSC
www.fsc.org
MIX
Paper from responsible sources
FSC® C005748

Printed on sustainably sourced FSC® paper.
Uses plant-based inks which reduces chemical emissions and makes this book easier to recycle.

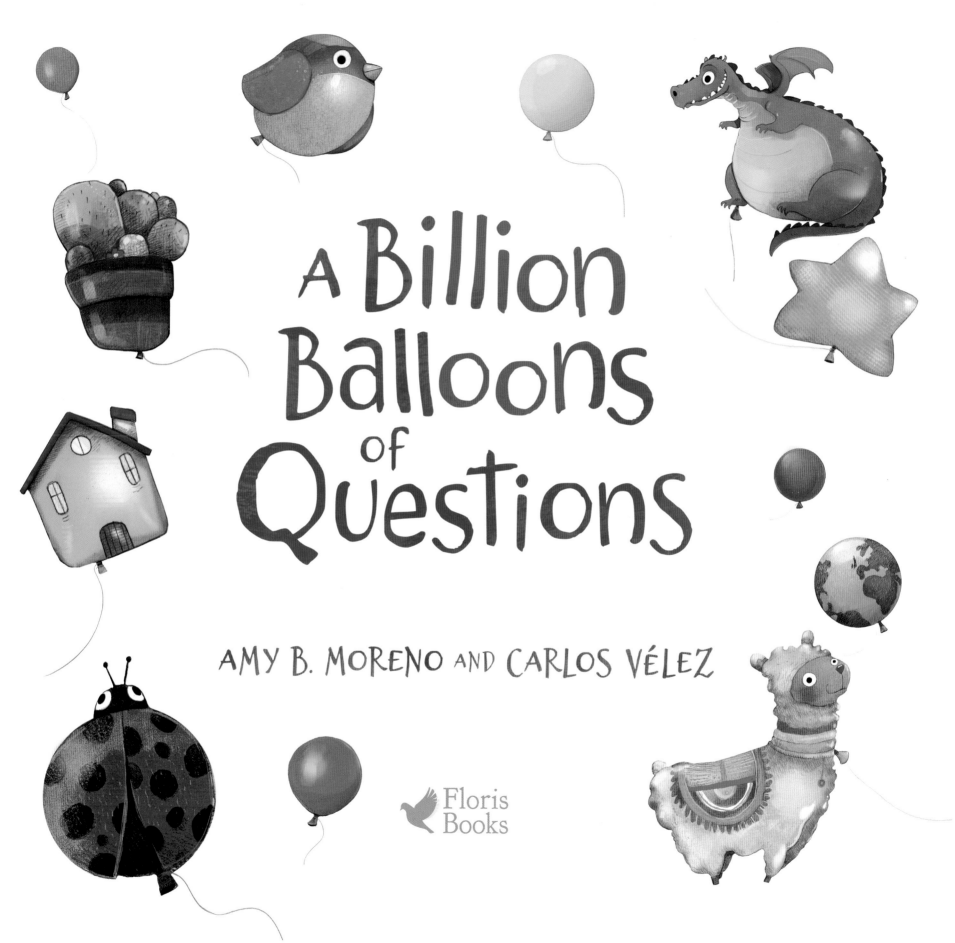

A Billion Balloons of Questions

AMY B. MORENO AND CARLOS VÉLEZ

Floris Books

HELLO! BUENOS DÍAS.

I'm Eva, and from the moment I wake up, my day is full of questions.

Mama says I have BILLIONS of questions, but really I have BALLOONS of questions. I carry them around with me all day, until I can find the answers.

My little brother, Sol, has sticky hands, a cute smile, and lots and lots of loud questions that he asks over and over again, like:

More toast for Sol?

¿Otra tostada para Sol?

More toast pleeeeaaaase?

More toast for Sol?

¿Otra tostada para Sol?

More toast pleeeeaaaase?

More toast for Sol?

¿Otra tostada para Sol?

Mama and Papá often put on That Face
and ask boring questions, like:

"How many times do I have to tell you to brush your teeth, Eva?"
And "¿Dónde están tus zapatos?"

Mama and Papá ask questions that feel all nice and cosy inside too, like, "Do you know how much I love you?"

I ask, "This much? ¡Así!"

COULD I MAKE A HUG THAT WOULD LAST ALL DAY?

Mama says, "Oh, much more than that, sweet pea."

Mrs McGregor asks learning questions like,
"What colour do we get if
we mix blue and yellow?"
And I say, "¡Verde!"

My friends ask exciting questions like,
"Do you want to play Superhero Animals?"
And I like that question, because the answer is always:
"¡Sí, sí, sí!"

My abuelita-on-the-screen in Peru has
sensible questions like:
"¿Cómo estás, Evita?"
So I say, "Muy bien, abuelita."
And she asks, "¿Te gusta la sopita?"
So I say, "Sí abuelita, me gusta la sopita."
My papá makes the best soup.

¿DÓNDE ESTÁ PERÚ?

Sometimes I listen to other people's questions all day long, while my bunch of balloons keeps growing...

WHAT CAN I DO ABOUT ALL THE PLASTIC IN THE OCEAN?

Until my head is full of big questions, small questions, dark questions and bright questions.

Mama and Papá can't always answer
my questions. I ask, "Papá, Papá, ¿qué..."
He says, "Estoy ocupado, Eva. ¡Uyyy!"

So I have to wait...

And I feel my question
get bigger... and bigger...
y más grande... y enorme...

Until I can't hold it in and...

But we often look for the answers together
(even if I have to wait for a bit).

And other times, when the grown-ups don't know, I can dream up the answers by myself.

DOES THE WORLD SPIN FASTER WHEN IT'S WINDY?

Some days, by bedtime,
all my questions have been
answered, and my balloons
have floated away.

Ahhhhh.

Other days, I tie my leftover balloons to the bedpost for the next day, then get tucked in and go to sleep.

Buenas noches.

Every morning there are more balloons waiting for me to explore.

DO BATS GET DIZZY HANGING UPSIDE DOWN?
¿QUÉ VAMOS A COMER HOY?
HOW DOES THE SUN RISE?

GLOSSARY

Español – Spanish

English – Inglés

abuelita grandma / granny

así like this

Buenas noches Good night

Buenos días Good morning

coco coconut

¿Cómo estás? How are you?

¿Cuál planeta es el más grande?
Which planet is the biggest?

¿Dónde está Perú? Where is Peru?

¿Dónde están tus zapatos?
Where are your shoes?

enorme enormous

Estoy ocupado I'm busy

¡guau, guau! woof, woof!

la Alpaca Mágica the Magical Alpaca

¿Los unicornios existen?
Do unicorns exist?

más grande bigger

Me gusta la sopita I like soup

muy bien very well / very good

¿Otra tostada para Sol?
Another piece of toast for Sol?

papá dad

¡PUM! POP!

¿Qué...? What...?

¿Qué hora es? What time is it?

¿Qué vamos a comer hoy?
What are we going to eat today?

¿Qué vamos a comer mañana?
What are we going to eat tomorrow?

sí yes

¿Te gusta la sopita? Do you like soup?

¡Uyyy! Ew!

verde green

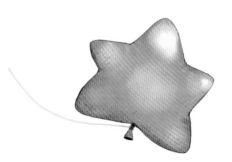

Amy B. Moreno is a poet and children's author from Scotland. She has worked with vulnerable children, young people and women, and in interpreting and translation. Amy speaks fluent Spanish and spent four years living and working in Peru. *A Billion Balloons of Questions* is her first picture book and was inspired by the experience of living in a bilingual household with her Scottish-Peruvian children. Amy currently lives in Edinburgh, Scotland.

Carlos Vélez is an award-winning illustrator from Mexico. He graduated from the Faculty of Arts and Design at the National Autonomous University of Mexico and is the illustrator of more than twenty children's books including *Sleeping with the Lights On*, *Three Lines in a Circle* and *We Belong*. Carlos currently lives in Coyoacán, Mexico.